# THE TIGER WHO LOST HIS STRIPES

ANTHONY PAUL

*ILLUSTRATED BY*

MICHAEL FOREMAN

Picture Lions

*An Imprint of* HarperCollins*Publishers*

General MacTiger was the most magnificent animal in the forest. He had splendid whiskers, flashing eyes and a stately walk. Most specially he had a thick silky coat with dazzling black stripes.

But one morning when the General took a look at himself in the river he had a horrible shock. He was all yellow! His stripes had gone!

This was a serious business. How could he be a tiger without any stripes? A tiger's whole tigerishness is in his stripes.

So what did he do? Did he sit down and cry? Certainly not! A tiger never cries. Did he get himself into a terrific thundering rage? Well, he almost did, but he stopped himself, remembering that he was General MacTiger, who was always dignified and stately.

So he kept calm, and said to himself, "By George, what a remarkable case of stripelessness! I must get to the bottom of it." And off he went to look for his stripes.

He looked in the long grass, in the reeds, in the bamboo groves. But not a sniff of those stripes could he find.

After hours of searching General MacTiger plodded home. By now he didn't feel at all like himself. He wondered if he had somehow been changed into a different animal altogether, some yellow stranger. He didn't like this idea at all.

Trudging sadly along, he saw something odd hanging from a branch, a sort of bag or basket made of stripes of dark stuff. Was it a wasps' nest? Was it a sock? General MacTiger looked, and he looked, and,

"MY STRIPES!!" roared General MacTiger.

From the basket-thing slid a flat head at the end of a long neck that wasn't exactly a neck. It was the python. In a dry whispery voice the python said, "Can't you make less noise?"

"Fury! Roar! Robber!" thundered the General.

"It's no good roaring," said the python. "Once I get my hands on something I hang on to it."

"But you haven't got any hands," said General MacTiger.

"So what," whispered the python, and slid back inside the basket-thing.

After a minute or so the General said, “Look here, python, what are you doing with my stripes? You must give them back to me.”

“What if I don’t?” said the python.

“If you don’t? — If you don’t — I’ll be very angry indeed!”

“How terrible,” said the python. “I’ll have to put my earplugs in. I hate loud noises.”

General MacTiger made a sound like a bath emptying. Then he said, “Earplugs? But you haven’t got any ears!”

“And you haven’t got any stripes,” said the python, and slid back inside the basket-thing. General MacTiger stood there with his mouth hanging open.

General MacTiger had a good think, then he called out, "Hey, python! What can I swap you for those stripes?"

"Swap?" said the python. "Well I like this house, but I suppose I might swap it for an even better one."

"What sort of better one?" said the General.

"Oh, a good strong one of elephant grass would do."

"Elephant grass?" said General MacTiger. "How can I build a house of elephant grass?"

"I don't know. Ask the elephants," said the python.

General MacTiger went down to the river to talk to the elephants, who were sloshing about there. They laughed heartily when they saw him. "Ho ho ho, you do look comic. Where are your pyjamas?" they shouted.

General MacTiger thought that even without stripes he looked a lot smarter than the elephants. But this was no time to say so.

So he just smiled politely and said, “I was wondering if you could help me with a little job. The thing is, I have to build a house for... ah, a friend of mine...”

“What friend?” said the Chief Elephant.

“Well, actually,” said the General, “it’s a snake I know. The... er...python.”

The Chief Elephant and all the other elephants laughed so hard that bunches of bananas came thumping down from the trees. Because they knew that the python had *no* friends, especially not the tiger.

"Very funny, I know," said General MacTiger. "But the fact is the python's got my stripes — you noticed I'm not wearing them today — and he'll only give them back if I build him a house. If you help me, maybe I can do something in return…"

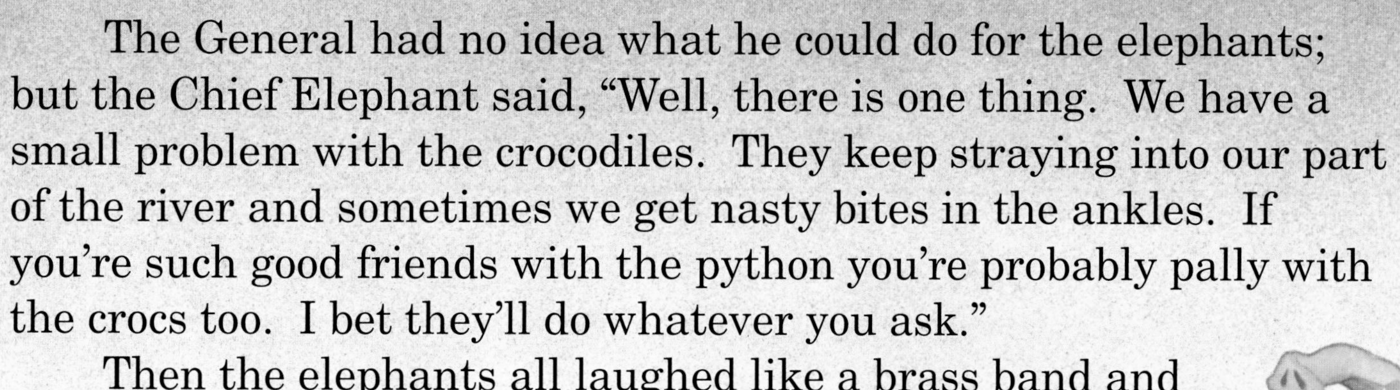

The General had no idea what he could do for the elephants; but the Chief Elephant said, “Well, there is one thing. We have a small problem with the crocodiles. They keep straying into our part of the river and sometimes we get nasty bites in the ankles. If you’re such good friends with the python you’re probably pally with the crocs too. I bet they’ll do whatever you ask.”

Then the elephants all laughed like a brass band and carried on squirting one another with water.

Standing well up on the riverbank, General MacTiger called down to the Grandmother of All the Crocodiles, who lay in the water like a log, with one pebbly eye open.

"Look here," said the General in an important voice. "You crocodiles have got to stay out of the elephants' part of the river, do you hear?"

In a deep creaky voice, the Grandmother of All the Crocodiles said, "Why?"

General MacTiger thought for a moment and said, "Well, you know what elephants are — great clumsy things. They're afraid of treading on you."

He felt pleased with this cunning answer.

The Grandmother of All the Crocodiles looked at him without blinking for quite a long time. Then she said, "If the elephants are so worried about treading on us, why don't *they* move?"

The General had no answer to that, so he huffed and puffed and said, "Well, they aren't moving and that's that."

The Grandmother of All the Crocodiles said in her creaky voice, "And if we move, what do we get?"

"Well, you won't get trodden on," said General MacTiger.

"That's what we shan't get. But what *shall* we get?" said the Grandmother of All the Crocodiles.

"Doom and despair," thought the General, "where will this business end?"

Just at that moment down came a shower of coconuts, bop bop bop, one on each crocodile. “It’s those monkeys again,” said the Grandmother of All the Crocodiles. “They love dropping coconuts on us. Big joke, ha ha. If you stop them, then we might move.”

“Stop the monkeys?” said the General.

“Right. Or else we stay put.”

And she fell silent and lay as still as a log. When a crocodile stays put it really stays put.

“Fine,” said General MacTiger, and bounded away. But he didn’t know how he was going to manage this. Monkeys never do what anyone asks them to do. To begin with, he couldn’t even see the monkeys, so he called out, “Monkeys! Are you there?”

A shower of nuts and ripe fruit landed on him, so he knew the monkeys were there. He wiped himself clean and he said, “Now listen, monkeys — ” But now the monkeys started chattering and squeaking so hard he couldn’t hear himself speak, so he stopped. He didn’t know what to say next anyway.

Now the General had another think, and when the monkeys’ noise had died down a bit he said to himself, “Let me see if my thinking is right,” and he called out, “Monkeys! Are you still there? I can’t hear you any more!”

Now as soon as they heard this, the monkeys shut up completely. Silence fell on the forest. It was so silent that all the animals stopped what they were doing to listen to the silence. Bears, boars, baboons, bees and beetles all stood still and listened. It was the most unnatural and unearthly silence.

Then in the middle of the silence there was a small sound. It was the sound of General MacTiger laughing. Then gradually all the other forest noises started up again.

"Monkeys!" cried General MacTiger. "The crocodiles want to thank you for your kind gifts of coconuts. Please keep sending them. They love coconuts. Thank you, dear monkeys."

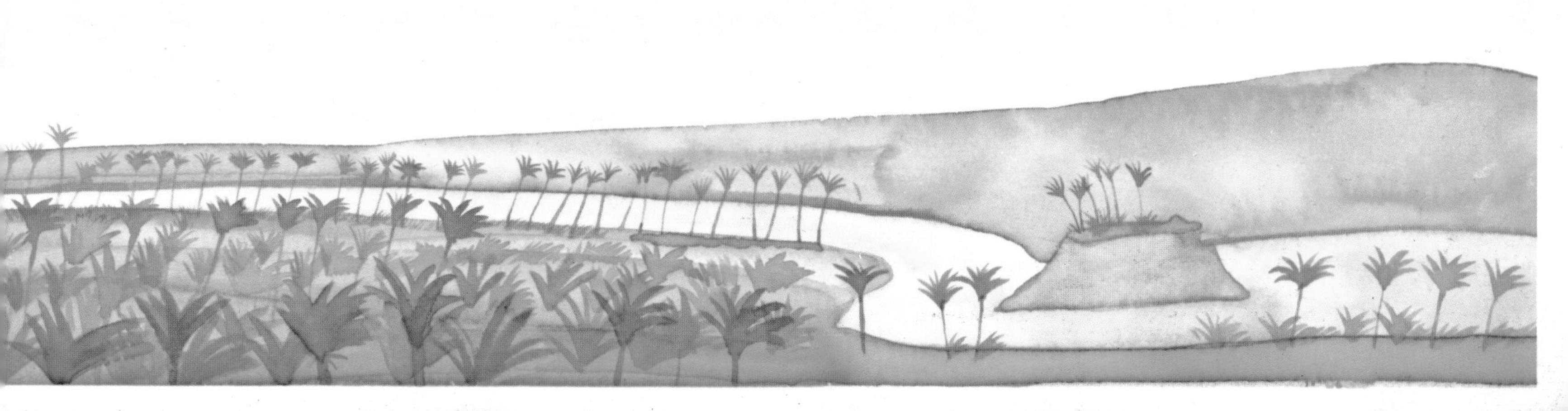

General MacTiger went to tell the crocodiles that the monkeys wouldn't be dropping any more coconuts on them. The Grandmother of All the Crocodiles opened her other eye and said, "How did you manage it?"

"Oh," said the General, "once you understand the monkeys they aren't so difficult."

So the crocodiles moved out of the elephants' water.

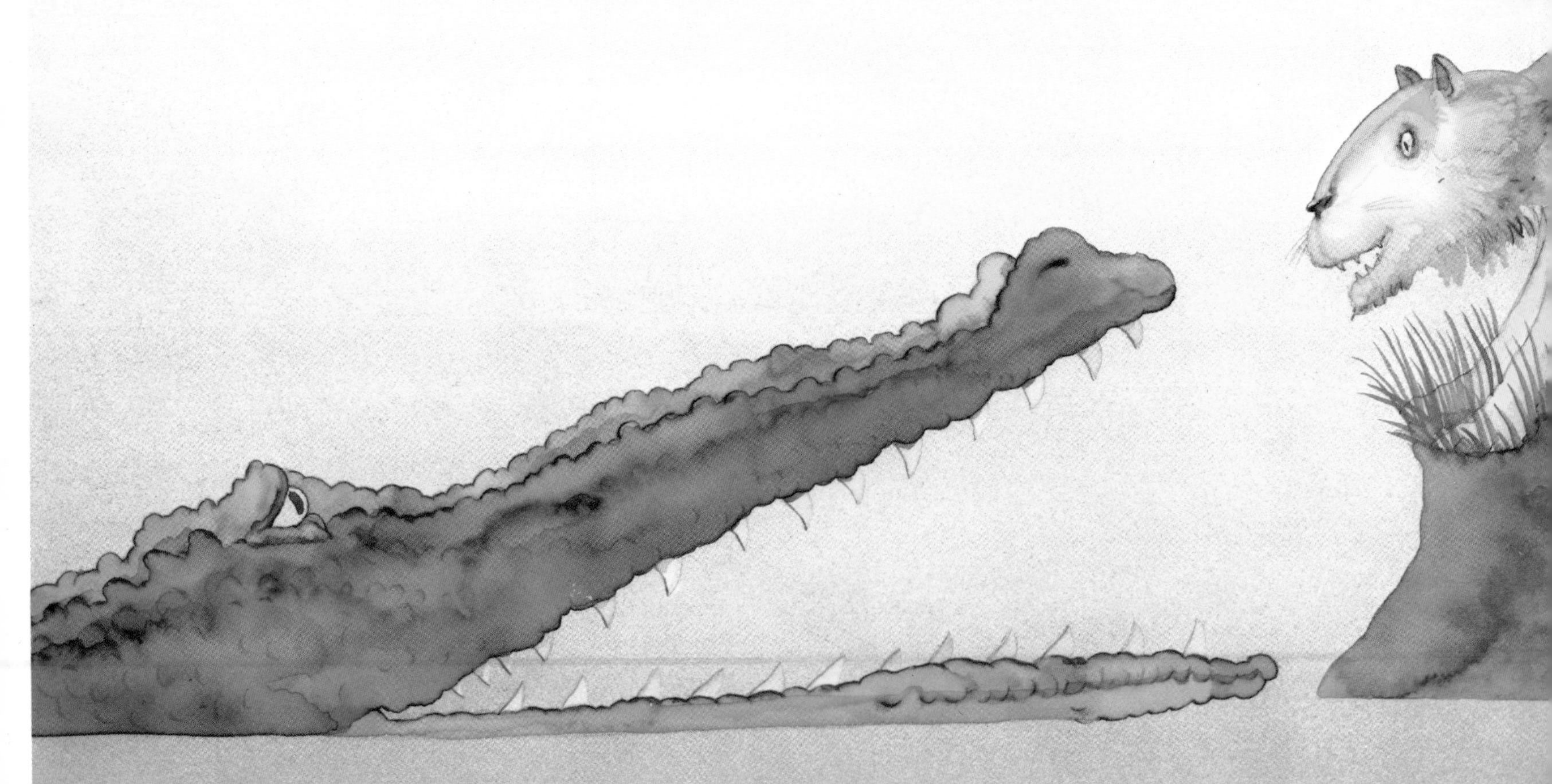

General MacTiger went to the elephants and said, “You see? The crocodiles have moved.” The Chief Elephant made a wheezy noise like leaking bagpipes, and said, “How did you manage it?”

“Oh,” said the General, “when you get to know the crocodiles they aren’t so crusty.”

So the elephants pulled up elephant grass and built a hut-thing. General MacTiger went to the python and said, “There’s your new house. Now give me back my stripes.”

The python liked the look of the hut-thing, so he slithered

into it and let General MacTiger's stripes fall to the ground.

Quick as a flash, General MacTiger untangled the stripes and put them back on. Now he felt exactly like himself again, and started jumping about like a tiger kitten, until he remembered that he was General MacTiger, who was always dignified and stately.

So he became tremendously stately, and paraded through the forest making sure that everything was just as it should be.